The Cat and the...

Dennis Lee

Illustrations by Gillian Johnson

KEY PORTER BOOKS

Wizard

To Max
GJ

Text copyright © 2001 by Dennis Lee
Illustrations copyright © 2001 by Gillian Johnson

National Library of Canada Cataloguing in Publication Data available upon request.

The publisher gratefully acknowledges the support of the Canada Council and the Ontario Arts Council for its publishing activities.

We acknowledge the financial support of the Government of Canada through the Book Publishing Industry Development Program (BPIDP) for our publishing activities.

Key Porter kids is an imprint of
Key Porter Books
70 The Esplanade
Toronto, Ontario
M5E 1R2 Canada

www.keyporter.com

An earlier version of this poem appeared in *Nicholas Knock and Other People*

Design: Peter Maher

Printed and bound in Canada

1 2 3 4 5   01 02 03 04 05

A senior wizard
Of high degree
With a special diploma
In wizardry
Is trudging along
At the top of the street
With a scowl on his face
And a pain in his feet.

A beard, a bundle,
A right-angle stoop,
And a hand-me-down coat
Embroidered with soup,
A halo of smoke
And a sputtery sound—
The only real magic
Magician around.

But nobody nowadays
Welcomes a wizard:
They'll take in a spaniel,
Make room for a lizard—
But show them a conjurer
Still on the ball,
And nobody wants him
Or needs him at all.

His bundle is bulging
With rabbits and string,
And a sort of machine
That he's teaching to sing,
And a clock, and a monkey
That stands on its head,
And a mixture for turning
Pure gold into lead.

He carries a bird's nest
That came from the Ark;
He knows how to tickle
A fish in the dark;
He can count up by tens
To a million and three—
But he can't find a home
For his wizardry.

For nobody, *nowadays,*
Welcomes a wizard;
They'll drool at a goldfish
Repaint for a lizard,
But show them a magus
Who knows his stuff—
They can't slam their latches down
Quickly enough!

In Casa Loma
Lives a cat
With a jet-black coat
And a spiffy hat,

And every day
At half past four
She sets the table
For twelve or more.

The spoons parade
Beside each plate
She pours the wine;
She serves the steak,
And Shreddies, and turnips,
And beer in a dish,
Though all she can stomach
Is cold tuna fish.

But a cat is a cat
In a castle or no,
And people are people
Wherever you go.

Then she paces about
In the big dining hall,
Waiting and waiting
For someone to call
Who won't be too snooty
For dinner and chat
At the home of a highly
Hospitable cat.

And every evening
At half past eight,
She throws out the dinner,

And locks the gate.

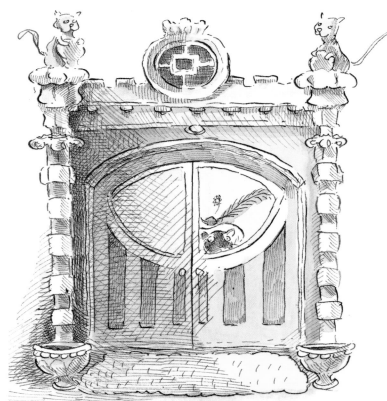

And every night,
At half past ten,
She climbs up to bed
By herself, again.

For a cat is a cat
In a castle or no,
And people are people
Wherever you go.

One day they meet
In a laundromat,
The lonesome wizard,
The coal-black cat.

And chatting away
In the clammy air,
They find they both like
Solitaire,

And merry-go-rounds,
And candle-light,
And spooky yarns
That turn out right.

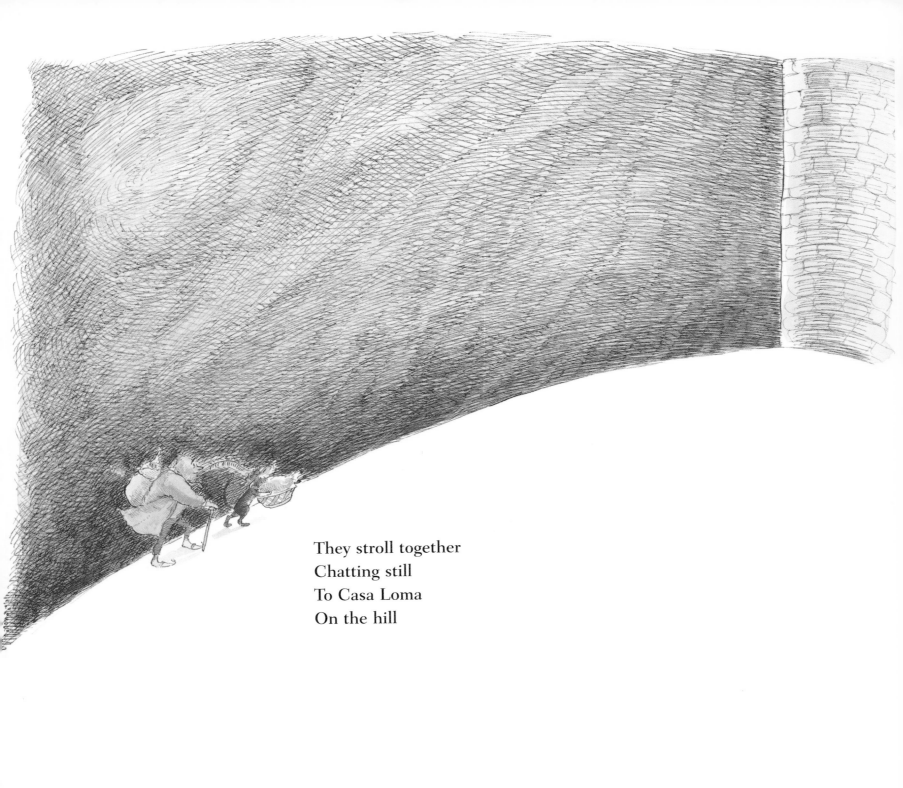

They stroll together
Chatting still
To Casa Loma
On the hill

And there the cat
Invites her friend
To share a bite,
If he'll condescend;

And yes, the wizard
Thinks he might—
But just for a jiffy
And one quick bite.

An hour goes by
Like a silver skate.
The wizard moves
From plate to plate.

Two hours go by,
Like shooting stars.
The cat produces
Big cigars

And there in the darkening
Room they sit,
A cat and a wizard,
Candle-lit.

At last the wizard
Takes the pack
From his creaking, reeking,
Rickety back.

He sets it down
With a little shrug,
And pulls a rabbit
From under the rug.

And before you can blink
He's clapping his hands,
And there in the doorway
A peacock stands!

Now he's setting the monkey
Upon its head,
He's turning the silverware
Into lead,

And counting by tens
From a hundred to four
And making a waterfall
Start from the floor,

And juggling a turnip,
A plate and a dish,
And turning them all
Into fresh tuna fish.

The cat is ecstatic!
She chortles, she sails
From the roof to the floor
On the banister rails,

And soon the whole castle
Is whizzing with things:
With sparklers and flautists
And butterflies' wings,

And all through the night
The party goes on—
Till it stops in a trice
At the crack of dawn,

And the wizard installs
His pack in a drawer,
While the cat tidies up
The living-room floor.

And as the sky
Is growing red,
They tiptoe up
The stairs to bed.

The wizard's snore
Is rather weird;
The cat is snuggled
In his beard—

Dreaming of tuna fish
End to end,
And rabbits, and having
A brand-new friend.

Perhaps you wonder
How I know
A cat and a wizard
Can carry on so?

Well: if some day
You chance to light
On Casa Loma
Late at night,

Go up to the window,
Peek inside,
And then you'll see
I haven't lied.

For round & round
The rabbits dance,
The moon is high
And they don't wear pants;

The tuna fish
Patrol the hall,
The butterflies swim
In the waterfall,

And high and low
With a hullaballoo
The castle whirls
Like a tipsy zoo!

And in the corner,
If you peer,
Two other figures
May appear.

One is dressed
In a spiffy hat:
The queen of the castle,
The jet black cat.

The other's a wizard
Of high degree.
The wizard is grinning.
The wizard is me.